Power Rangers Jungle Fury

Enter... The Wolf!

Adapted by Slade Stone from the original script by William Carter
Illustrated by Scott Neely and Candace Schinzler-Bell

Published in 2010 by Creative Edge, LLC.

Printed in the U.S.A.

The evil power of Dai Shi has once again been unleashed upon the world. Three brave kung fu students have been selected and trained in the coastal city of Ocean Bluff to combat Dai Shi and his Overlords. RJ, their master, has coached the teens well. These are the Jungle Fury Power Rangers.

"With the strength of a Tiger!" calls Casey. "Jungle Fury Red Ranger!"

"With the speed of a Cheetah!" calls Lily. "Jungle Fury Yellow Ranger!"

"With the stealth of a Jaguar!" calls Theo. "Jungle Fury Blue Ranger!"

Spirits of the Jungle— Power Rangers Jungle Fury!

In a secret temple, on a cliff above Ocean Bluff, an angry, taunting roar resounds. From out of a blue mist, the Overlord Grizzaka emerges. With his Zokado power, he blasts a hole in the rock wall to reveal...

"Zokado! Awaken my mighty guards!" commands Grizzaka.

Two of the warriors begin to glow! They fly up into the air, landing next to their master.

"I serve only you, Overlord!" says one warrior.

"Speak and it shall be done," says the other.

"My two guards," replies Grizzaka, "you will destroy the entire city of Ocean Bluff. Then my full army shall take over the world!"

The two guards are sent into the city to terrorize the citizens. With each scream and cry for help, the guards gather energy. "Scream all you want," they sneer. "We feed on your fear!"

The guards shoot their energy beams into the sidewalks—shattering them! But as they aim at the buildings, they are confronted by...

"Attack!" calls the Yellow Ranger.
"Let's see if you can handle my spin!" adds the Blue Ranger.

But the strength of the guards is great. Lily is thrown to the ground, and Theo is easily swatted away.

"Whoa," says Lily. "These guys are powerful."

"Yeah," says Theo. "They're as mean as they are ugly."

The guards advance, raising their staffs as the two teens struggle to get to their feet. The villains prepare to strike—but are knocked off their game by the Red Strike Rider!

"Attack mode!" calls Casey. "Come on, team! The four of us can handle these goons!"

"Four...?" asks Theo.

With the added courage of the Wolf, the Rangers battle the mighty guards.
"Wolf Power!" commands RJ, electro-shocking one guard.
"I'll take that!" declares Lily, wielding her Jungle Mace with accuracy.
"Jungle Tonfa—baton battle!" calls Theo.
"Booster Claw—go!" yells Casey, swiping at the enemy.
But the Zokado power is strong in the guards. They resist the Rangers' fury!

"Okay, guys. Time to ramp this up," says the Wolf. "If you bring out the Claw Cannon, I'll boost it with my Wolf Beam."

"Good idea, Wolf Master!" agrees Lily.

"Jungle Fury Claw Cannon—fully charged—fire!"

"Beam Blast!" howls the Wolf.

The Wolf Beam boosts the power of the blast from the Claw Cannon—reducing the guards to rubble!

But from afar, Grizzaka roars, "How dare they! Zokado Power—arise!"

The crumbled guards blast up from the ground— forming huge Monster Guards!

"Uh-oh..." says the Wolf. "This game just got a little uneven."

"There's two of them," says the Blue Ranger.
"We're going to need everything we've got!"
"It's Megazord time!" cries the Red Ranger.
Together the three teens call:

Animal Spirits Unite as one!

The three Zords of the great cat spirits leap up and join forces to become the Jungle Master Megazord, operated from within by the Rangers.

But it is no match against the two Monster Guards. The Wolf Ranger watches with fury as the Megazord suffers blow after blow.

"I think it's time for another surprise Wolf entrance," muses RJ. "Jungle Fury— Wolf Spirit Mode!"

The great Wolf Zord appears! Piloting the Zord, the Wolf Ranger commands, "Wolf Zord! Spin Fury!" A blur of purple power spins toward a towering guard—only to be repelled by the guard's staff. Again the Wolf Zord attacks—but again it is repelled!

"There's only one way we can defeat these guys," declares the Wolf Ranger. "Animal Spirits—Arise!"

The three teen Rangers watch with amazement from within the Jungle Master Megazord cockpit. The Wolf Zord replicates itself and then becomes three Zords—Wolf, Tiger, and Jaguar!

"Awesome!" cheers Theo.

"That's nothing!" cries the Wolf Ranger. "Let's see how they cope with two Megazords. Animal Spirits—Unite!"

JUNGLE PRIDE MEGAZORD!

The Monster Guards are no match for the two Megazords. This game of two-on-two is a slam dunk for the Rangers! Using triple-boost blasts and spin-mode attacks, they defeat the enemy and free the city!

"RJ, you really kicked it in gear! Thanks!" says Casey.
"Yeah! Great instincts!" agrees Theo.
"And great entrance!" adds Lily.
"No prob, guys. It was a *blast* to help," grins RJ.